P9-BZS-399

Susan Hood

Just Say BOO!

illustrated by
Jed Henry

HARPER
An Imprint of HarperCollinsPublishers

Just Say Boo!

 For information address HarperCollins Children's Books, a division of HarperCollins Publishers, 10 East 53rd Street, New York, NY 10022.
www.harpercollinschildrens.com

Library of Congress Cataloging-in-Publication Data is available.
ISBN 978-0-06-201029-2 (trade bdg.) — ISBN 978-0-06-201030-8 (lib. bdg.)

Typography by Dana Fritts
12 13 14 15 16 SCP 10 9 8 7 6 5 4 3 2 1 ❖ First Edition

For Maria
—S.H.

For the Taylors, who celebrate Hallo*week*,
because one hallowed eve is never enough
—J.H.

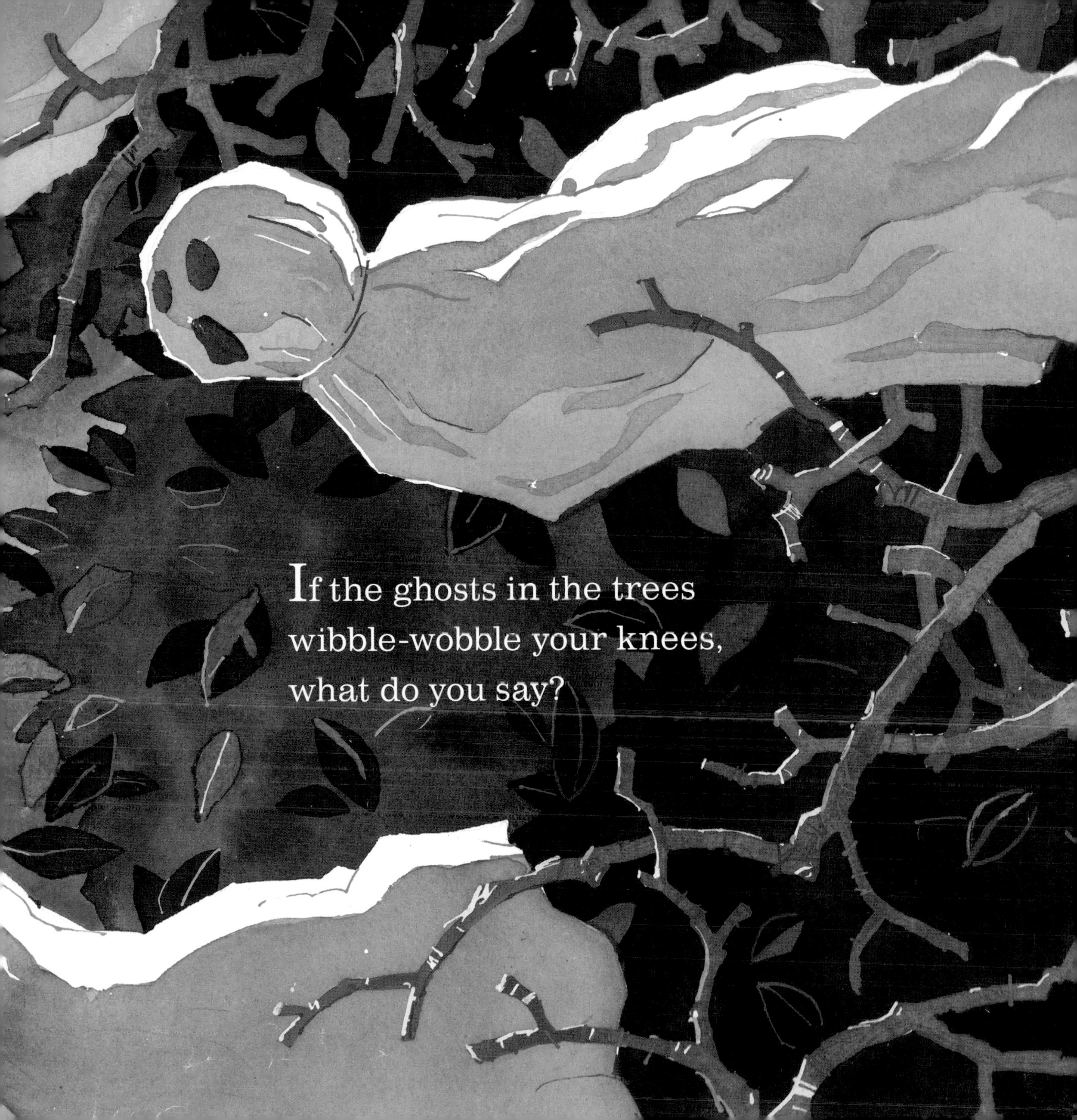

If the ghosts in the trees
wibble-wobble your knees,
what do you say?

BOO!

If a yip and a yowl
make you shiver and scowl,
what do you say?

BOO!

If the wind whirls and whines
as it whips through the pines,

what dooooo yoooooou saaaaaay?

Boooooooooooooo!

If wet, shriveled leaves
try to tug on your sleeves,
what do you say?

EWW!

If a flickering grin
gets under your skin,
what do you say?

BOO!

If a skeleton groans
as she rattles her bones,
what do you say?

BOO!

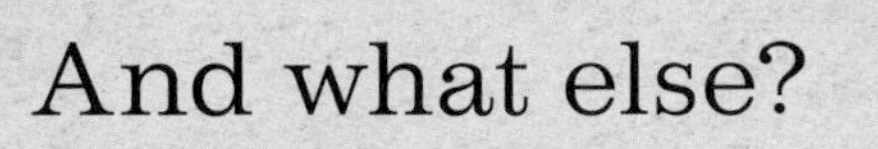

And what else?

TRICK

or
TREAT!
And
what
else?

"Thank you!"

Now . . . if faint footsteps fall
by your neighbor's stone wall,
what do you say?

BOO!

If a smug, ugly bug
tries to give Mom a hug,
what do you say?

BOO!

If three dinosaurs roar
when you open your door,
what do you say?

BOO!

BOO!
BOO!

BUT . . .
if the little one cries,
please help dry his eyes
and teach him to just say

BOO!